Julie Bridges
1984

OCT 2023

W9-CGK-860

Christopher Discovers a Secret

Originated and produced
        by Roi Tauer
Story by
        Donna Merrick
        and
        Ginnie Clark
Pictures by
        Robert Clark

Published by Nascence

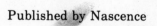

WATERTOWER BOOKS

DIVISION OF CHILDRENS PRESS

MANITOBA

Copyright © MCMLXXVII by Roi Tauer

Cover: ARTFORM DESIGNS, INCORPORATED
J. GELICK

Fleeing from the frozen marsh
  In Northern Manitoba,
A group of moose began to march
  To Ely, Minnesota.

Their life was hard—from hoof to mouth—
To find more food, they traveled South.

The trip was long, the snow was deep.
The smallest moose was half asleep.

His legs were short, his antlers tall;
He really made no speed at all.

Christopher A. Moose, The Third (III)
Kept struggling on without a word.
He longed to stop and ease the strain.
But Christopher would not complain.

At last his dad, a moose of might,
Called for a halt to rest that night.

The little moose—the one named Chris—
Said, "Dad, I'm glad you thought of this.

"These heavy antlers on my head
Make it a joy to go to bed."

Snug in a snowbank they all drifted off
To sleep with their antlers like branches aloft.

But during the night
A blizzard so mighty
Covered Christopher up
With a snowy white nighty.

He slept through it all,
Hidden somewhere below—
Out of sight 'cause his antlers
Were covered with snow.

Next day when he woke
And raised up his head,
He climbed slowly out
Of his wintery bed.

The morning was quiet,
No sound in the air—
Not a mooseprint
Could Christopher
See anywhere.

"Where have they gone?
Where can they be?

"Why has my family
Forgotten me?"

Poor Chris was so frightened,
So lost and alone,
Without friends and family
Before he had grown.

With head bowed low, he chanced to see
The shadow of a giant tree . . .

Chris looked again, more carefully.
"Why, that's no tree," said Chris,
"THAT'S ME!"

It made him brave, though he was small,
To know his antlers were so tall.

So off he went, he knew not where,
To find his folks someplace out there.

He traveled far, and farther still,
Through snow and ice in winter's chill.

For miles and miles he searched for food;
He thought some tree bark would taste good.

But all the trees were miles behind,
And twigs were all that he could find.

At last he saw some friendly men
All dressed up snug in walrus skin.

They looked so strange—
Where could he be?

"North Pole," they said.
"I'm lost," said he.

But then he thought,
  I think it's here
That Santa lives
  Throughout the year.

Chris heard a noise up in the sky,
And there went Santa flying by,
Training his reindeer, left and right,
Practicing for the perfect flight!

But Santa's sleigh still lacked a rack
To safely hold his Christmas sack.

The elves were working to repair
The damage from last season's wear.

The reindeer took a turn too fast,
And Santa's sack went flying past.

Chris knew the toys would all be smashed
And dashed to help before they crashed.

He leaped to catch them, jumping high.
SMALLCAPS SUCCESS! As they went sailing by
In Santa's pack, he caught the sack.
His antlers were a perfect rack!

But why was he not coming down?
He wondered with a worried frown.

He floated high above the ground
For quite some time, and then he found
That he was gliding high in flight.
An AIRBORNE moose! Oh, what a sight!

His antlers were like wings on planes,
His tail, a rudder, which explains
The reason he could glide so high
On updraft breezes in the sky.

He twirled his ears, then turned around
And floated smoothly to the ground.

"Well! What is this?" Old Santa said.
"You caught my sack upon your head!
You're not a reindeer, that's quite clear.
YOUR antlers spread from THERE to HERE!"

"No," Chris replied, "I'm not a deer,
But I just learned a secret here:
My antlers are so very wide,
And I'm so small, that I can glide!

"I didn't know it right away,
But now I'll practice every day
That there's a wind or steady breeze
To lift me up above the trees.

"I'm Christopher A. Moose, The Third (III).
I've lost my family. Have you heard?

"They got up early weeks ago
While I was sleeping in the snow.
They didn't know, they couldn't see,
The snow completely covered me.

"So on they went and never guessed
I wasn't traveling with the rest.

"I got confused and turned about—
I headed North instead of South.

"But gliding high will show me more
Than I have ever seen before,
And that will help me find my dad
And all the other friends I had."

"Good luck," said Santa. "Thank you, too!
The toys are all as good as new—
Not one broken, not one cracked,
Because you did your gliding act."

"Christopher, listen—do you hear
A far-off bellow? Turn your ear."
Christopher listened. The sound was sad.
Somehow he knew it was his dad.

He cocked his ear to hear the sound
And raised his head toward higher ground—
And there, upon a snowy mound,
His dad stood looking all around.

"Here I am, Dad," Christopher cried.
His heart was thumping hard, inside.
The startled father stood quite still,
Then galloped wildly down the hill.

Old Santa beamed—it was a treat
To know the two again would meet.